First published in Great Britain in 1985
by Methuen Children's Books Limited,
11 New Fetter Lane, London EC4P 4EE
First published in Sweden in 1984
by Raben & Sjogren Bokforlag, Stockholm
under the title Spelar min lind
Text copyright © 1959 Astrid Lindgren
Illustrations copyright © 1984 Svend Otto
English text copyright © 1985 Patricia Crampton

Printed in Denmark

ISBN 0 416 52060 X

My Nightingale is Singing

ASTRID LINDGREN

Illustrated by Svend Otto
Translated by Patricia Crampton

Methuen Children's Books

Long ago, in the days of poverty, there was a poorhouse in every parish, where all the poor of the parish lived: the old who could no longer work, the sick, the spent and destitute, the half-crazed, and homeless children whom no one would take care of – all of them gathered together in that place of sighs which was the poorhouse.

There was one in Scunton parish too, and to it one day came Maria, who was eight years old. Her father and mother had died of consumption and the Scunton farmers were afraid she might be carrying the infection. They would not take her for pay in the usual way and that is why she went to the poorhouse.

It was on a Saturday evening in early spring and all the paupers in the poorhouse were sitting by the window staring down the road, which was their only entertainment on Saturday evenings. There was not much to see: one belated farmer's cart coming home from the town, a couple of crofter's lads going pike-fishing, and Maria, with her bundle of clothes under her arm. Their eyes widened at the sight of her.

"Poor me, going to the poorhouse," thought Maria as she stood on the steps outside. "Poor me."

She opened the door, to be met by
Pompadella, the old woman who laid
down the law in the poorhouse.

"Welcome to the house of poverty,"
said Pompadella. "It's crowded already
in here and it's not going to get any
better – though you'll not take up
much room, a skinny little thing like
you."

Maria stared at the floor.

"We don't want any jumping about
in here," said Pompadella, "you'd best
know that from the start."

The paupers sat round the walls,
gazing sorrowfully at Maria.

"Who would want to jump about in
here?" she thought to herself. "Not me,
nor anyone else either."

She knew the Scunton paupers
already, because they went round the
parish every day with their begging
bags, begging a crust for the sake of
holy charity. Yes, she knew them all.
There was Fuggy, the dirtiest man in
the parish, whose name was used to
frighten the children although he was
kind and decent and never harmed a
soul; there was Joey Squint, whose
brains had been touched by God, and
Georgie Porgie who could eat ten blood
puddings and still ask for more; there
was the Gaffer with his wooden leg and
Hen-Helen with her bleary eye, Little
Pin and Dearie-Dearie and Spotty
Anna, and over them all there was big,
powerful Pompadella, appointed by the
parish to reign over the poorhouse.

Maria stood at the door, looking round the misery and want of the poorhouse, and thinking that this was where she would have to spend her childhood until she was old enough to go into service. Her heart was heavy, she could not imagine how she could live where there was neither beauty nor fun.

Her own home had been poor, but there had been both beauty and fun in it: the apple tree outside the window, when it flowered in spring, and the clumps of lily-of-the-valley, the cupboard with the painted roses, the big blue candlestick, Mother's brown loaves fresh from the oven, the kitchen floor on Saturdays, newly scoured and covered with chopped juniper twigs — oh, her home had been all beauty and fun before the sickness came.

But here in the poorhouse the dirt was enough to make you weep and outside the window there was nothing but a bleak potato field, no flowering apple trees and no clumps of lily-of-the-valley.

"Poor me," thought Maria, "now I am the littlest pauper in Scunton and all the beauty and fun are over."

That night she slept in a corner on the floor, but first she lay awake a long time, listening to the paupers, two in a bed, snoring and sniffing. There they slept after the drudging and trudging of the day, Fuggy and the Gaffer, Joey Squint and Georgie Porgie, Hen-Helen and Dearie-Dearie, Little Pin and Spotty Anna. But Pompadella lived alone in the attic, sharing her bed with nothing but the bugs.

Maria woke up towards morning and in the cold grey light of dawn she saw the hordes of bugs parading up the walls. They were going home to their nooks and crannies now, but the next night they would return and grow fat on the paupers.

"If I were a bug I'd leave this place," thought Maria. "But perhaps bugs don't want any beauty and fun, just so long as there are four beds with eight paupers in them and a little pauper on the floor."

From where she lay Maria could also see under the beds, where the paupers hid everything that they could scrimp and scrape from the inhabitants of the parish: a bit of bread here, a few peas and oats there, a scrap of meat, a few coffee beans and a kettle of old coffee dregs.

One by one the old people woke up and began to squabble about who should be allowed to boil his coffee first; they crowded round the open hearth with their kettles, grumbling and grousing, but when big Pompadella came in she elbowed them aside and set her own three-legged coffee pot over the fire.

"A drop for me and my helper first," said Pompadella.

Overnight she had decided that it might be a good idea to have a helper when she went begging. Surely, for the sake of holy charity, the parishioners would not allow an innocent child to starve to death. But Maria sat staring sorrowfully over the rim of her coffee cup at all the want and misery of the poorhouse, trying to find one single solitary sign of beauty. But there was nothing, nothing at all.

So she began to walk the parish
with Pompadella, visiting all the
farms, begging for bread.
Pompadella was pleased with her
little helper and passed her the
best of all they had begged, and
in the evening she boasted of
Maria to the other paupers who
had no help.

But Maria had a kind heart and tried to be a helper to them all. When Hen-Helen could not knot her laces with her twisted old fingers, it was Maria who knotted them for her; when Dearie-Dearie dropped her ball of wool it was Maria who fetched it for her and when Joey Squint was frightened of the voices inside his head it was Maria who calmed and comforted him. But she could not comfort herself, because for someone who could not live without beauty there was no comfort to be had.

One day she and Pompadella went to the parsonage, where the parson's wife gave them bread for their begging bag and porridge at the kitchen table for the sake of charity. But something else happened that day, something wonderful. Then and there, in the parson's kitchen, Maria received something beautiful for her heart's comfort. Someone was reading a story aloud to the parson's children in the next room and as Maria sat at the table eating her porridge and thinking of nothing in particular, words flooded through the half-open door, words so beautiful that she began to tremble.

She had never known before that words could be beautiful, but now she knew, and they sank into her soul like morning dew on the fields in summer. Oh, she wanted to hide them inside her till the end of time and never forget them, but even as she reached the poorhouse with Pompadella, they vanished. Only a few of the most beautiful were left, and these she repeated over and over again to herself:

My linden plays,
my nightingale is singing.

In the glory of those words, all the want and misery of the poorhouse vanished, though she had no idea why this should be so.

Life went on. There was no end to the Scunton paupers' sighs and moans, their hunger and need, their bitter waiting. But Maria had her words to comfort her heart and they helped her to endure. There were many hard things to be seen and heard in the poorhouse. There sat Dearie-Dearie with her ball of wool, winding yarn from one ball to another all the hours of the day, ceaselessly, uselessly, and when she thought of all the yarn she had wound and knitted in her youth she wept in silence, as Maria saw . . . *my linden plays, my nightingale is singing* . . . And Joey Squint was frightened and heard voices inside his head, so he banged it against the wall and begged and pleaded with the other paupers to change heads with him, which made them all laught except for Maria . . . *my linden plays, my nightingale is singing* . . . And when evening came to the poorhouse and there was no candle left to light, the paupers sat on their beds staring into darkness and memories, mumbling and sighing, whining and whimpering, and Maria heard them . . . *my linden plays, my nightingale is singing* . . .

But as time went by she was no longer satisfied with the words alone. They grew into a longing inside her which was with her night and day. Now she knew what she wanted: a playing tree, a singing nightingale, just like the queen in the fairytale. The thought gave her no rest and it came to her that she should plant a seed in the potato field and see if a linden tree might not grow there.

"If only I had a seed," she thought, "then I would soon have a linden tree, and if I had a linden tree, I would soon have a nightingale, and if I had a nightingale there would be nothing but fun and beauty in the poorhouse."

She asked Pompadella as they were walking together between the fields:

"Where can you find linden seed?"

"On linden trees in autumn," said Pompadella.

But Maria could not wait till autumn. Nightingales sing and linden trees play in springtime and the days of spring were running out like water through pebbles. If she could not find a seed soon, it would be too late.

She woke up early one morning before all the rest, perhaps because of the bugs or perhaps because of the sun peeping in through the poorhouse window. As she lay there scratching, her eyes followed the ray of sunlight under the Gaffer's bed and there she saw something lying on the floor, something small and round and yellow. It was only a pea that had rolled out of the Gaffer's threadbare bag, but it came to her that she might use it instead of a seed. Perhaps just this once, God in His goodness might let a linden spring from a pea.

"Only believe," thought Maria and she went out to the potato field and dug a hole in the ground with her bare hands, where she planted the pea which was to grow into a linden tree.

And then she began to believe. She believed so hard, every morning when she woke up, listening with her whole soul for a playing linden and a singing nightingale in the potato field, but she heard only the paupers snoring in their beds and the sparrows twittering outside.

"It will take a little time," thought Maria, "but only believe!"

And she looked forward to the beauty and fun there would be in the poorhouse. One day, when Joey Squint was crying over his voices and banging his head against the wall, she told him about the loveliness that was to come.

"When the linden plays and the nightingale sings you won't hear your voices any more," said Maria.

"Are you sure?" asked Joey Squint.

"Yes, only believe," said Maria.

Joey Squint was beside himself with joy and began to believe straight away, listening every morning for a playing linden and a singing nightingale in the potato field. But one day he told Geogie Porgie about the loveliness that was to come and Georgie burst out laughing and said that if a linden tree grew in the potato field he would cut it down.

"We've got to have potatoes," said Georgie, "and in any case there won't be no linden tree."

Joey Squint went to Maria with tears in his eyes.

"Is it true what Georgie says, that we've got to have potatoes and there won't be no linden anyway?"

"Only believe," said Maria, "and when the linden tree plays and the nightingale sings, Georgie won't need potatoes any more."

But Joey Squint was still worried.

"When is the tree coming?"

"Perhaps tomorrow," said Maria.

That night she lay awake a long time, believing harder than she had ever believed before. Surely the strength of her belief would burst the crust of the earth and make linden trees spring up in all the woods and groves in the world!

She fell asleep at last and did not wake up until the sun was high in the sky. She knew at once what had happened, for all the paupers were standing at the window, gaping in wonderment. Sure enough, a linden tree was growing in the potato field, the prettiest little tree you could wish for. It had green, delicate leaves, beautiful little branches and a straight, fine trunk. Maria was so happy that she thought her heart would fly away . . . sure enough, the linden tree had come!

Joey Squint was beside himself with joy and even Georgie stopped laughing and said:

"A miracle has happened in Scunton sure enough, there *is* a linden tree!"

Yes, there was a linden tree, but it did not play. Not at all. There it stood, silent, without stirring a leaf. God in His goodness had made a linden spring from a pea, oh, why had He forgotten to give it breath and life?

Out on the potato field all the paupers had gathered, waiting to hear a playing linden and a singing nightingale as Maria had promised, but the tree was silent. Maria shook the little trunk despairingly. Without a playing tree there would be no nightingale either, as she knew.

All day long Joey Squint sat on the poorhouse steps, listening and waiting, but in the evening he came to Maria with tears in his eyes.

"You promised it would play, you promised a nightingale would come."

And Georgie Porgie no longer thought the tree was a miracle.

"What's the good of a tree that doesn't play?" he said. "Tomorrow I'll cut it down. We've got to have potatoes."

Maria cried, for now she saw no hope of having anything beautiful in the poorhouse.

The Scunton paupers went to bed, no longer waiting for a nightingale. They waited only for the bugs, and the bugs sat in their nooks and crannies, waiting for them.

So the spring night fell silently over Scunton parish.

But Maria lay in her bed in the poorhouse, unable to sleep. At last she got up and went out into the potato field. The spring sky stood bright and clear above the dark house, above the silent tree and the sleeping village. No one but Maria was awake, yet she could feel that the night was full of life. The spirit of spring was alive and near in leaf and flower and grass and tree, there was breath and life in every plant and blade. Only the linden tree was dead. There it stood in the potato field, beautiful, silent and dead.

Maria laid her hand on its trunk and suddenly she felt how hard it was for the
linden tree to be the only thing without life and to be unable to play. It came to her
that if she could give her breath to the dead tree, life would stream into the little
green leaves and the delicate green branches and the linden tree would begin to
play for sheer joy so that all the nightingales would hear it in all the woods and
groves on earth.

"Yes, then my linden would play," thought Maria, "then my nightingale would sing and there would be beauty and fun in the poorhouse."

Then she thought: "But I wouldn't be there any more, because you can't live without breathing. I would live on though, in the linden tree, I would live in my narrow green house to the end of time and the nightingale would sing for me through the evenings and the nights of spring. It would be wonderful."

No one in all the parish was awake, so no one can say for certain what happened there by Scunton poorhouse one spring night long ago. They know only one thing for certain . . . that all the paupers were awakened at dawn by the beauty of the music from the potato field; a playing linden and a singing nightingale woke them to a day of joy and gladness. The linden tree played so beautifully, the nightingale sang so wondrously that there was beauty and fun in the poorhouse.

Maria had gone, never to return. They all missed her and wondered what had become of her, but Joey Squint, who was not too bright, said that when the linden tree played, he could hear only one voice in his head, whispering:

"This is Maria!"